The Case of the Secret Skeleton

by James Preller

illustrated by Jamie Smith
cover illustration by R. W. Alley

SCHOLASTIC INC.
New York   Toronto   London   Auckland   Sydney
Mexico City   New Delhi   Hong Kong   Buenos Aires

*This book is dedicated to my creative
daughter, Maggie, who helped me with ideas
for the story. Thanks, Mags, but I'm
not sharing the money.*

—JP

ISBN-13: 978-0-545-15040-8
ISBN-10: 0-545-15040-X

Text copyright © 2009 by James Preller
Illustrations copyright © 2009 by Scholastic Inc.

12 11 10 9 8 7 6 5 4 3 2 1   9 10 11 12 13 14/0

Printed in China
First printing, September 2009

Can you help Jigsaw Jones solve a new kind of mystery? This book comes with a Spy Ear clue finder. When you read the story and see this symbol

on a page, push the matching button on your Spy Ear. You'll hear a secret audio clue that doesn't appear in the book.

Good luck with the case. And keep your Spy Ear in a safe place. You don't want it to fall into the wrong hands!

CONTENTS

CHAPTER ONE
The Riddle

It was a plain white envelope. There was no stamp on it. No writing, not a single word. I held the envelope up to my nose and sniffed. Nothing special about it — except that somebody had stuffed it inside my desk.

I glanced around the classroom. Bobby Solofsky was busy making gross sounds with his armpit. Solofsky had the manners of an orangutan, but there was no denying it — he had talent. My best friend, Mila Yeh, chatted near the cubbies

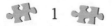

with Helen Zuckerman. Ralphie Jordan laughed, Stringbean Noonan hummed, and Joey Pignattano secretly munched on candy corn.

No one looked at me.

No one seemed to care what I was doing.

So I tore open the envelope.

Inside, there was a white sheet of paper. It had been neatly folded, like freshly ironed clothes.

The message was typed. And it was addressed to me:

DETECTIVE JONES,

YOUR MISSION WILL BE TO SOLVE THE RIDDLES AND FOLLOW THE CLUES. YOU WILL EITHER FIND THE ANSWER TO THE MYSTERY . . . OR FAIL.

TICK-TOCK, THE CLOCK BEGINS. YOU HAVE THREE DAYS TO COMPLETE YOUR TASK. HURRY, BEFORE IT'S TOO LATE.

OH, YES, THE FIRST CLUE: *WHO GOES INTO A CAFÉ AND ORDERS A GLASS OF LEMONADE AND A MOP?* YOU'LL FIND THE NEXT CLUE IN ITS BONY GRIP, SOMEWHERE IN THIS BUILDING.

I tucked the note inside the envelope and shoved it into my back pocket. Again I scanned the classroom for watchful eyes. Ms. Gleason was at her desk, talking with Bigs Maloney. She always let us have a few extra minutes to get settled after recess. If someone in class put the note in my desk, they were playing it cool. But who could it be?

Thrum, thrum, thrum. My heart pounded louder than usual. My knees itched. I always feel that way at the start of a mystery. After all, I'm a detective. For a dollar a day, I make problems go away. I've found missing hamsters and stolen bicycles. I've faced marshmallow monsters and walking scarecrows. And I make good money, too. It keeps me stocked with new jigsaw puzzles. That's how I got my name — Jigsaw Jones. I love solving puzzles. It doesn't matter what they look like, all puzzles arc the same. You solve them one piece at a time.

So I sat at my desk, puzzling over that first clue.

Who goes into a café and orders a glass of lemonade . . . and a mop?

CHAPTER TWO
Laser Tag Blues

I called an emergency meeting of the Jigsaw Jones Detective Agency. That's a fancy way of saying I invited Mila over for help. You have to say it "My-la" — not "Me-la" — or else she gets mad. It makes Mila crazy when people say her name wrong.

Mila and I are partners. We solve mysteries together. Sometimes I think Mila could solve mysteries without my help. But today, I needed hers. Besides, it was more fun that way.

I waited in my tree
house. I could hear Mila
coming from a distance.
She was singing, loud and
off-key. The tune was
"Happy Birthday," but
the words were new:

> *"Happy mystery . . . to solve,*
> *Happy mystery . . . to solve,*
> *Happy mystery, oh, Jigsaw,*
> *We have a riddle to solve!"*

It wasn't the best song Mila ever made up.
She sang like a sick walrus. Maybe I even
said so.

"Why so grumpy?" Mila asked.

"I'd rather not discuss it," I said.

"Okay."

"Okay?" I said. "That's it? You aren't
curious *why* I'm in a bad mood? What kind
of detective are you?"

Mila shrugged. "You told me you'd rather not discuss it."

"Mila, I might have *said* that, but I didn't *mean* it!"

"Okay, I'll try again," Mila said. "Why so grumpy?"

"My birthday's coming up," I said. "Your song reminded me."

"Oh, I had forgotten about your birthday. But that's good news, Jigsaw. What's the problem?" Mila asked.

"I wanted to have my party at Ike and Tina's Laser Tag and Putt-Putt Emporium — but my parents said no."

"Really?"

"Yeah, my father says we've got to tighten our belts this year," I explained. "That means cutting back on spending."

Mila pulled on the strands of her long black hair. She was a good listener. That made her a good detective — and a good friend.

"Everybody has their party at the Putt-Putt Emporium," I said. "Everybody — except for me."

"But you'll still celebrate your birthday, right?" Mila said.

"Sure, we'll have cake and presents," I said. "I'll pick my favorite dinner. But let's face it, Mila. Laser Tag would have been way cooler."

Mila shrugged. "I'd rather have a sleepover, watch a DVD, and paint my toenails."

Oh, brother. Time to change the subject. "Here's the note."

Mila examined the page carefully. "This was typed on a computer," she observed.

"That's what I figured. Handwriting would be too easy to trace."

"Well," Mila said, "did you figure out the riddle? Who orders lemonade and a mop?"

I told her I didn't have a clue. "All this

thinking about lemonade is making me thirsty."

Mila agreed.

"Let's go inside," I said. "We'll work in the kitchen. I think better on a full stomach."

CHAPTER 3
Mop

I poured two cups of grape juice.

Mila studied the note. *"Hmmm,"* she murmured.

"Is that a good '*hmmm,*' or a bad '*hmmm*'?"

"It's a weird '*hmmm,*'" Mila said. "Who would send this — and why?"

"No idea," I said. "But we should start by solving the riddle."

"Okay, who orders lemonade?" Mila said. "That's easy, someone who's thirsty."

"But what about the mop?"

Mila frowned.

"Let me see that paper again." I grabbed for the riddle.

"Wait, Jigsaw!" Mila pulled it away.

That's when I knocked over Mila's cup. *Splash! Drip, drip, drip*. A purple puddle formed on the floor.

Slurp! Rags, my dog, hurried over to lap it up.

"Sorry, Mila," I apologized.

"It's okay, Jigsaw. No use crying over spilled grape juice."

"Look at Rags," I said. "He's better than a mop."

"That's it!" Mila exclaimed. "That's why the person needs a mop — he spills the lemonade."

"A clumsy person," I said. "Like Bigs

Maloney, maybe. He's always knocking things over and stepping into puddles."

Mila shook her head, dissatisfied.

I scratched my head and looked around the room. My mom had already put up Halloween decorations even though it was three weeks away. She was like that. My mom couldn't wait for the holidays. There were ghost candles, skeletons on the wall, spiders and spooky witches on the windows.

Skeletons.

"What about a skeleton?" I asked.

"A skeleton?" Mila murmured. "Could be. If he drinks the lemonade —"

"— it would spill on the floor —"

"— and you'd need a mop!" we both exclaimed.

Mila pointed to the last sentence of the note. She read it out loud. *"You'll find the next clue in its bony grip, somewhere in this building."*

"Bony grip!" I exclaimed. "*Skeleton* has to be the right answer."

My brothers Daniel and Nick barged into the kitchen. Nick headed straight for the snack drawer. "Hey, Mila," Daniel said. "What's up, Worm?"

That's what he called me. *Worm.* All of my three older brothers liked teasing me.

Rags leaped up on Nick, nosing in the snack drawer. "What happened to Rags? His face is purple."

"Grape juice," Mila said.

"He cleaned up a spill," I explained.

Daniel looked at the floor. "That's not good enough, Jigsaw. Mom will freak — grape juice will stain the floor. You better clean it up yourself."

Typical Daniel. Sometimes he acted like my boss instead of my brother.

"Yeah, you need a *mop*," Nick added. He slammed the drawer shut. "Don't they ever

go shopping anymore? There's nothing good to eat."

Nick was ten years old, but he ate like a rhino.

Mila kicked me under the table. Hard. It totally hurt.

She slid a finger across her nose. That was our secret signal.

"What?" I asked.

"Nick said *mop*," she whispered.

"So?"

Mila's eyes widened. She lifted her shoulders, then let them drop.

"Do you think he — ?"

Mila zipped her lips. She turned to Nick and asked, "Did you find anything yet? I'm hungry, too."

CHAPTER 4
Let's Take a Ride

It was a little strange. I mean, Nick saying "mop" and everything. I don't think we even *owned* a mop.

Mila and I sat on the front stoop. I bounced a tennis ball on the blue slate walkway.

"Maybe Nick was giving us a hint," Mila said.

"You think *he* sent the note?" I asked. "How?"

"Don't know yet," she said. "He goes to our school. It's *possible* — that's all I'm saying."

I tossed the ball to Mila and picked up a pen. I wrote in my detective journal:

THE CASE OF THE SECRET SKELETON

Mila looked over my shoulder. "Nick is our first suspect."

"Just because he said 'mop'? I don't know, Mila."

"It's like you always say, Jigsaw. Everyone is a suspect . . . and anything is possible."

So I wrote:

NICK JONES — SUSPECT #1

"We have to find that skeleton," I said. "Got any bright ideas?"

"Yes, I do," Mila said, beaming. "Remember that time we talked to Mr. Copabianco in the janitor's storage room?"

"Yeah, so?"

"There was a skeleton in the corner of the storage room," she said.

There was? I didn't remember. You'd think a guy might remember a skeleton in a closet.

"Why would Mr. Copabianco have a skeleton?" I asked.

Mila shrugged. "Lots of teachers keep stuff in there. Maybe it's for science class or something."

"Maybe," I murmured. But my mind was already working on a different problem.

"If Nick's a suspect, we'll have to spy on him."

"That's easy enough," Mila said.

I shook my head. "Nope. Nick knows most of my tricks. Last week he found me hiding under his bed."

"We'll have to try something new," Mila said.

"That's right," I agreed. "And I know just the person who can help us — Reginald Pinkerton Armitage the Third. Put on a clean pair of socks, Mila. We're going for a ride."

Reginald Pinkerton Armitage III was the richest kid in town. Reginald once tried to make it as a Secret Agent Man. He got

into more jams than a box of blueberries. And I always helped him out. Reginald owed me a favor.

He loved trick gizmos and gadgets. Reginald had spy scopes and tiny cameras. But when it came to real detective work, he didn't have a clue. So he gave up the Secret Agent business. Reginald said I could borrow his gadgets anytime. And right now was anytime.

When we pulled up to his house, Mila whistled. "His house is gigantic."

I did push-ups on the doorbell. *Gong-dong, ditty-gong, ditty-ditty-ding, BONG-DONG, ditty-DONG* echoed through the vast house.

The heavy door swung open. "Jigsaw Jones! Mila! What a splendid surprise!" exclaimed Reginald. He wore a bow tie and a crisp white shirt. His hair was slicked back. "To what do I owe this pleasure?" Reginald's right pinky pushed back a pair of round eyeglasses.

I shoved my hands in my pockets. "Business, Reg. We're working on a case."

He slapped his hands together. "Delightful!"

"Yeah." I grimaced. "I guess you could say that. I wouldn't, but you can."

Reginald smiled. "You crack me up, Jones. You really do. Outstanding!"

"That's the problem, Reg," I said. "We are 'out standing.' And it's getting cold out here. How about you invite us inside?"

CHAPTER FIVE

Reginald Pinkerton Armitage III

Reginald Pinkerton Armitage III apologized for his lack of manners. With a sweep of an arm, he invited us into the house.

He looked at my shoes and cleared his throat.

"Don't worry, I remember the rules," I said. "We even wore clean socks." Mila and I kicked off our shoes.

I told Reginald that I was hoping to borrow one of his fancy gadgets.

"Ah, detective work," Reginald purred. "Follow me."

Reginald walked down a long hallway. We tagged along behind, our stocking feet sliding on the tile floor. We made two lefts and a right at an old grandfather clock. Reginald stopped before a white door. "I'm awfully glad to see you two. My auntie Griselda is visiting from La Jolla. She's very proper. I have to be on my best behavior. It can be a little . . ." His voice trailed off.

"Boring?" Mila suggested.

"Indeed, quite right, rather," Reginald confessed.

"Is that why you're all dressed up?" Mila asked.

Reginald nodded. "We're attending the opera tonight."

"Oh, joy," I groaned.

"I think it sounds exciting," Mila said. "You're lucky, Reginald. Not everybody gets to do stuff like that."

I counted my lucky stars.

Reginald pushed open the white door. "Come into my research room."

The room looked like a laboratory. Counters lined the walls. They were covered with all sorts of spy gear.

I picked up a silver toy gun. "What's this?"

"Do be careful, Jigsaw. That shoots laser beams."

I aimed at a wall and pulled the trigger.

A thin beam of red light shot out. "It's just a flashlight," I muttered. "Kid stuff."

"You might prefer this." Reginald offered me a pen. "Go on, click it."

A powerful light shone out from the tip.

"Cool, and easy to carry, too," I said, pocketing the small flashlight.

"We need to spy on Jigsaw's brother," Mila explained.

"Ah, I have just the thing." Reginald picked up a small black object. "Father brought this back from the Far East. I daresay it's exactly what you need."

He told us that it was a high-tech listening and recording device. Reginald called it a Spy Ear. "You can be in the next room and it will sound as clear as a bell."

"We'll take it," I said.

"Splendid!"

"Splendid?" I repeated.

"It means —"

"I know what it means, Reg," I interrupted. "It's a ten-dollar word that means 'great.'"

Reginald's shoulders drooped.

"Don't be rude, Jigsaw," Mila said. "I like the way Reginald speaks. He has . . . *style*."

Reginald seemed to stand a little taller after that. I decided to keep my big yap shut. I could be a real wise guy sometimes.

On our return trip to the front door, I switched on the Spy Ear. I wanted to see how well it worked for myself. Suddenly, I heard talking outside the front door. I peeked through the window curtains and saw the family's butler speaking with the chauffeur.

Push Button (1)

Reginald was right. I could hear them perfectly. The Spy Ear just might help solve this mystery.

I turned to Reginald. "Thanks a lot, Reg. You really helped us out."

"Totally," Mila chimed in. "You're a true friend."

Reginald's cheeks turned pink. He murmured, "Gee, I don't know what to say."

"Splendid," I said. And we all laughed.

CHAPTER SIX

The Skeleton Clue

The first thing in school the next morning, Mila and I went to look for Mr. Copabianco, the janitor. He was a short man with thick eyebrows and a bristly mustache. But where could he be? I turned on the Spy Ear and heard an unmistakable sound.

Push Button (2)

Mr. C always had a huge ring of keys hanging from his belt. I could hear them jingle and jangle. We followed the sound until we spotted him down a hallway.

"Hello, Mr. Copabianco!" Mila said.

"Good morning, Mila, Jigsaw!" he greeted us. "Happy Thursday!"

I asked him if he had a minute.

"Sorry, busy, busy, busy," he said. "Come see me later." He hurried away.

Usually, I liked school. I really did. But sometimes it got in the way of detective work. When there are mysteries to solve, nobody wants to review spelling words.

Ms. Gleason kept us working all morning. It danced on my nerves. All I could think about was that spooky skeleton. Finally, she announced, "All right, class. Please clear off your desks. It's such a beautiful

day outside. You may take a short break to get some fresh air."

I asked Ms. Gleason if I could go see Mr. Copabianco.

"Is anything the matter?" she asked.

I didn't want to go into details. But I didn't want to lie, either. So I said, "I'm working on a case."

Ms. Gleason leaned forward. "Another mystery?"

I nodded.

"Is Mr. Copabianco . . . a suspect?" she asked.

"Until the case is solved," I said, "everyone is a suspect."

"Oh, my!" Ms. Gleason's eyes grew large. She glanced out the window. "Please hurry along, Jigsaw. You've got five minutes."

I had one last question for Ms. Gleason. "When we're all in the lunchroom, is Room 201 empty?"

"Yes," my teacher answered. "I usually go to the teachers' lounge."

"Uh-huh. Is the classroom locked?"

"Locked? No. People are free to come and go. Mr. Copabianco sometimes comes in to empty the garbage baskets. Mail is delivered. That kind of thing."

I hurried to the janitor's room. It was really just a big closet that Mr. C shared with a bunch of mops, boxes, and school supplies.

I knocked on the door. "Anybody home?"

No one answered. I looked up and down the empty hallway. I was alone. So I pushed open the door.

It was dark. Fortunately, I came prepared. I pulled out Reginald's miniflashlight. It cast a narrow beam of light. I scanned it across the room. I saw a desk, cluttered shelves, boxes upon boxes, and two eye sockets in a creepy skull.

Good thing my shoes were tied. Or else I might have jumped out of my socks. It was the skeleton. I ran the flashlight down the skeleton's arm. And there it was in his bony grip — a rolled-up piece of paper.

The next clue.

I plucked the paper from the skeleton's grip. "You won't be needing this," I mumbled.

Then I got out of there faster than you could say, "Trick or treat."

Hanging out in a dark closet with a skeleton was not my idea of a good time.

I nipped into the bathroom and unrolled the page:

CONGRATULATIONS, YOU SOLVED THE FIRST CLUE.

HERE'S A WORD YOU'LL NEED — SATURDAY.

AND HERE'S ANOTHER CLUE: *WHAT TIME IS IT WHEN TWO HANDS REACH FOR THE SKY?*

CHAPTER SEVEN
Reach for the Sky

I sat at the end of a long lunch table with Mila, Ralphie Jordan, and Joey Pignattano. We were talking about the latest clue.

"I'm telling you, it's definitely from *Toy Story*!" Ralphie said. "Woody says it. Don't you remember? *'Reach for the sky!'*" He held out an imaginary gun and pointed it at me.

"So you think that's what it means?" I said. "Like I'm being robbed or something?"

"I don't know. . . ." Mila sounded doubtful. "Don't forget the first part of the question. *What time is it?*"

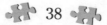

"You guys are wrong," Joey interjected. He pointed to my potato chips. "Are you going to eat those, Jigsaw?"

I slid my tray in front of him. Between eager chomps, Joey continued. "It's like when you score a goal in soccer. You throw your arms up in the air to celebrate."

"So it's time . . . to celebrate?" I asked.

"How about those cookies?" Joey asked Ralphie. He slowly reached for Ralphie's dessert. "Are you going to eat all — "

"Touch one of my cookies," Ralphie warned, "and I'll jab your hand with a plastic spork."

Joey looked pained. "Don't get snippy, Ralphie. I was just asking."

"Let's start from the beginning," Mila suggested. "The note gave you a word — Saturday. The next part is about *time*."

While Mila talked, I noticed Bobby Solofsky at the end of the table. He

whispered something to Eddie Becker. I turned on the Spy Ear and . . .

Push Button (3)

The noon bell exploded in my ears.
I switched off the Spy Ear — and it hit me.

"Look at the clock." I pointed. "What time is it, Joey?"

"It's time for recess," he said.

"But *how* do you know?" I asked.

Joey shrugged.

"Both hands are . . ." Joey's eyes grew large. He grinned.

". . . pointing to the sky," Ralphie chimed in.

"It's twelve o'clock!"

"Nice work, Jigsaw!" Mila said. She leaned back in her chair. "It seems like this . . . weirdo riddler person . . . wants you to be somewhere on Saturday, at noon."

"Or midnight," Ralphie said.

Midnight? Yipes. Noon was more likely. I hoped. "But where?" I wondered.

"It's going to take detective work," Mila announced. "I'll ask around. See if I can find any witnesses. Somebody might have seen the riddler sneak into the classroom."

"Good thinking," I said. "I'm tired of chasing these riddles. It's time we figured out who's writing the notes."

I told Mila that I'd look for Mr. C. "He's a suspect," I said.

"Good old Mr. C?" Joey asked.

"He has the keys to every classroom," I said. "The skeleton was in *his* storage closet."

I wrote in my journal:

MR. C — SUSPECT #2

Bobby Solofsky called down to our end of the table. "What's up, *Theodore*?"

I snapped the journal shut. Solofsky was a stone in my shoe. He was the spinach on my plate, the rain on my camping trip, and the only kid who called me Theodore. Solofsky did it just to bug me. And it worked. I was bugged.

"Are you going to have a birthday party this year, Theodore?" he asked. "I had mine at —"

"— Ike and Tina's Laser Tag and Putt-Putt Emporium," I said through gritted teeth. "Yeah, yeah, you already told us all about it. Hey, how do you know my birthday's coming up?"

"Huh?" Solofsky said. He tilted his head, thinking, then snapped his fingers. "It's on the bulletin board. Everybody knows when the next birthday is coming up."

Solofsky was right. Ms. Gleason posted all the birth dates for the whole year. But it was weird that he brought up my birthday out of the blue. Maybe he had heard that I *wasn't* having a party this year. Solofsky might have wanted to rub it in.

"I always check the bulletin board," Joey admitted. "I like to be prepared for class parties and surprise cupcakes."

Everybody laughed at that. Joey was the king of cupcakes. But I still kept an eye on Solofsky. Had he been lying?

Most people are honest. They want to tell the truth. So when they lie, they give themselves away. In the detective business, it's called a *tell*. A liar won't look you in the eyes. He'll blink a lot. Or touch his mouth or nose. I didn't notice anything strange about Solofsky. He was acting normal. But then again, Solofsky was a good liar. It was impossible to be sure. The most important question a detective can ask is, *Why?*

Why would Solofsky lie?

I couldn't think of a good reason — yet. But even so, it was time to round up the usual suspects. I wrote in my journal:

SOLOFSKY — SUSPECT #3

CHAPTER EIGHT
One Last Try

I didn't talk much on the bus ride home. Mila sat beside me, reading one of the Puppy Place books by Ellen Miles. This one was called *Noodle*. Even though Mila could read big books, she still liked to breeze through short ones now and then.

It was a strange case. What did I have so far? A creepy skeleton and a couple of clues: *Saturday* and *noon*. Today was Thursday, almost four P.M. I did the math in my head. Something was going to happen in forty-four hours. But what? And where?

Mila closed her book. "Are you okay, Jigsaw?"

"Yeah, sure."

"What were you thinking about?"

"The case, I guess," I told her.

"You'll figure it out, Jigsaw. You always do."

"Thanks," I said. "You doing anything after school today?"

Mila tightened her lips. "Piano lesson,"

she said. "We've got a big recital on Saturday afternoon."

As a detective, I liked to take action. Make things happen. But there wasn't much I could do. I had to sit back and wait for the riddler to make a mistake.

Things got worse at dinner. In the Jones house, dinner was like a game of tackle football. We had my parents, Grams, and five hungry kids. It got a little rough sometimes. Once I got an elbow in my ear.

"So, Jigsaw," my mother said. "Have you decided what you'd like for your birthday dinner? It's only a week away."

"I don't care. Pizza, I guess," I said.

"You don't have to decide this minute," she said.

I shrugged. "It's not a big deal. Whatever."

My father leaned forward in his chair. "Jigsaw, your mother is offering to cook a special dinner for you. She'll even bake a cake. You should be grateful."

I looked from my father to my mother to Grams. "Bobby Solofsky had his birthday party at Ike and Tina's Laser Tag and Putt-Putt Emporium."

"That place is awesome!" Daniel and Nick exclaimed. They high-fived over a bowl of string beans.

"Their pizza rocks, too," Hillary added.

"Laser Tag?" Grams asked wonderingly.

"Modern stuff," my father clucked to Grams. "Nothing is simple anymore. The parties just get bigger and bigger."

"Dad, it's my *birthday*," I said.

"Look, Jigsaw," he said. "When I was a boy, we didn't have birthday parties. We didn't even have *birthdays*. Nobody knew how old they were until it was time to vote."

He was pretty pleased with his joke.

"It's not funny, Dad," I complained. "Everybody has parties at Ike and Tina's."

"Everybody?" my mother asked.

I ticked the names off on my fingers. "Danika, Joey, Bigs, Bobby —"

"That's enough," my father stated. I could tell from his voice that he meant it. "I'm sorry, Jigsaw. But we're not everybody. It's just not in the budget this year." He stabbed at a piece of chicken and shoved it into his mouth. "End of story."

There was an awkward silence. Then all the kids asked to be excused.

"Hillary, it's your night to clear the table," my mother said. "And your turn to load the dishwasher, Jigsaw."

CHAPTER 9
All Ears

Don't get the wrong idea. Even though I'm the youngest, I'm not spoiled. I understood that my parents were right. Money doesn't grow on bushes. But I didn't have to be happy about it.

I mean, I *loved* Laser Tag.

"Yes, Mary Lou . . . um-hum, Mary Lou . . . yep . . . almost done."

I didn't know what was worse, loading the dishwasher or listening to my sister, Hillary, blab into the phone. I didn't even know

why she was on her cell phone in the kitchen. She usually talked (and talked, and talked) in her room.

I glanced around the kitchen. The counters were wiped down. The dishes put away. All done. I left to the sound of Hillary's voice: "Um-hum . . . don't worry . . . I'm sure he'll be close soon. . . ."

I was a detective on a mission. I crept soundlessly down the hallway. The door to my brothers' room was shut. I heard faint voices. Daniel and Nick were inside. They had always shared a room.

I silently turned the knob to my room door. Careful not to make a sound, I lifted Reginald's Spy Ear from my sock drawer. I tucked in the earbud, switched it on, and listened. It was amazing how well I could hear.

"Shh, not so loud, he might hear us." It was Nick's voice.

"He's probably still washing the dishes," Daniel answered.

"But you know how sneaky he is," Nick said. "Let's whisper."

I smiled to myself. I heard every word perfectly.

"Dad was pretty harsh tonight." I was surprised to hear Billy's voice. My oldest brother didn't usually hang out in their room. Something was up.

"Anyway," Billy continued. "Did you guys want to chip in for a present or what?"

"No," two voices chimed. Giggling followed.

"Funny, guys," Billy said. "But we have to do something. He's not having a party this year. Mom and Dad don't have money for big presents. Hillary says she'll pay a few bucks. Maybe we could get him, like, I don't know . . ."

Push Button (4)

What? That is the most boring present ever. A goldfish? A goldfish?! Fish just . . . swim in circles. Then they die and you have to flush them in the toilet bowl. They do a few more circles and that's it. Gone, good-bye.

A goldfish would be the worst present ever.

"Great idea!" Billy exclaimed.

"And it's cheap, too!" Nick said.

I flicked off the Spy Ear. I didn't want to

hear any more. My birthday wasn't going to be much this year. No party. No great presents. But at least I'd have a new goldfish.

Glub, glub, glub.

Flush.

CHAPTER 10
Phone Call

I was slurping down a bowl of cereal when the phone rang.

"Who could be calling at eight in the morning?" my mother wondered.

She didn't have to wonder long. "It's for you," she said.

Me? Who would call on a Friday morning? Could it be another clue? Just in case, I decided to record the call.

I switched on the Spy Ear and reached for the phone. "Hello?"

The voice didn't sound human. It was

more like a robot. Or
the way a robot might
sound — if robots, like,
made phone calls.

Push Button (5)

"Hello? Hello?" The line went dead.

My mother looked at me. "Who was that, hon —?"

Hillary barged into the kitchen, breathless. "I don't have any clean socks!"

"I'll alert the National Guard," my mother ho-hummed.

"Mom! My bus leaves in, like, zero minutes!"

My mother sighed. "Okay, okay. Follow me."

As she turned to leave, I said, "Mom, I'm going to take Rags for a walk. Okay?"

"Rags? Now?"

"Yeah, he just seems, you know . . ."

Rags had already heard the magical word, *walk*. He stared up at me, wild hope in his eyes.

"Make it quick," she said. "Your bus comes in half an hour."

The corner of Birch and Vine was three blocks away. Rags and I ran the full distance. The tree was famous in our neighborhood. First of all, it was a good climbing tree. We were always on the lookout for those. Plus, there was a big hole in it, probably once a home for a small animal. I reached in and found a piece of paper.

Everybody in the whole wide world
Likes to have a little fun –
Mysteries, puzzles, and games.
Please forgive the run-around.
And when you solve the clues
Remember one final thing :
Keep following blue balloons!

It was a poem, sort of. I couldn't make any sense of it. Where was the clue? *Keep following blue balloons?*

There was no time to figure it out. I shoved the paper into my back pocket. "Come on, Rags. Let's go."

At the bus stop, I told Mila about my morning adventures. She was just as confused as me. "What did the caller say again?"

I handed the poem to Mila. "The voice said, *You will find the next clue inside the tree on Birch and Vine.*"

Mila read the poem in silence. "I don't know, Jigsaw. I guess we should keep our eye out for blue balloons."

The bus pulled up, and we were on our way.

Nothing much happened in school. I tracked down Mr. C. But once again, he was in a big hurry to be somewhere else. "Sorry, Jigsaw. We'll talk next week, after" — he looked away, scratched his nose — "the weekend."

Hmmm. *Strange.* I decided to go for it. "Do you know anything about blue balloons?" I asked.

He looked at me in surprise. "What? Balloons?"

Mr. C had no idea what I was talking about.

I thanked him and left. I didn't know what to think. At one point, Mr. C seemed to be lying. But by the look on his face, I was sure he didn't know anything about the balloons. That meant he hadn't written the poem.

Still, I wondered if this was a two-man job.

CHAPTER 11
A Little Help

There was still the problem of the poem.

And the fact that it was driving me crazy.

We had all talked about it at lunch, at recess, and even during P.E. The poem was okay, as poems go. But it didn't *lead* me anywhere. A good clue takes a detective to the next step. A detective follows clues, the way a hound follows a scent. But for me, the trail was cold.

Mila suggested that the poem might be a code. I tried them all: substitution codes, alternate letter codes, checkerboard codes, every code I could remember.

"Maybe you guys are thinking too hard," Joey said. "When I'm stuck, I just ask Ms. Gleason. It is faster than thinking — and easier, too."

By the end of the school day, I was desperate. "Please read this," I said to Ms. Gleason. I set down the note on her desk.

Everybody in the whole wide world
Likes to have a little fun -
Mysteries, puzzles, and games.
Please forgive the run-around.
And when you solve the clues
Remember one final thing :
Keep following blue balloons!

"Oh, Jigsaw, you've written an acrostic poem. Nice job!"

I may have mumbled something like, "Wha — ?" Or grunted, "Huh?"

"An acrostic," she said, smiling. Ms. Gleason ran her finger down the first letter of each line. "We studied acrostic poems in September, remember? It's a poem where special letters spell another word or phrase. Usually the special letters come at the beginning of each line."

I was speechless. There it was, right in front of me, but I hadn't seen it:

ELMPARK

I scribbled it in my journal, adding a space

where the two words had been stuck together. ELM PARK.

Elm Park!

It wasn't far from where I lived!

I returned to my seat. What else did I have? I jotted down the answers to all the clues.

Saturday, Noon, Elm Park
Follow the blue balloons

"Jigsaw? Jigsaw?"

I looked up. Ms. Gleason was standing beside my desk. The room was empty. "You'll miss your bus."

"My bus?"

"The bell rang two minutes ago," she said. "Everyone's gone."

I shut my journal, grabbed my backpack, and flew out the door. I was so frazzled, I forgot to thank Ms. Gleason. Oh, well. I'd bring in an apple on Monday.

Acrostic. Go figure. I guess homework can help a detective after all!

CHAPTER 12

Blue Balloons

Saturday morning, I saw sparrows chirping outside my window. I heard my brothers talking in their room. And I felt my dog, Rags, slobbering on my pillow.

Gross.

Nobody likes waking up in a puddle of slime.

But I didn't let that ruin my day. I was excited. Today, I'd solve the mystery. *Twelve o'clock at Elm Park. Just follow the blue balloons. . . .*

I shoved Rags to the side — he was a total

bed hog — and picked up Reginald's Spy Ear. Once again, I listened in to my brothers' room.

Push Button (6)

I thought back to the first time I spied on my brothers. Could they have known I was listening?

I had been in the kitchen, washing dishes. Hillary was talking on her cell phone. I remembered thinking that it was strange. She usually talked in her bedroom. Even now, I could hear her voice: ". . . almost done . . . he'll be close very soon . . ."

Hillary had been spying — on me! She was probably talking to Billy. He also had his own phone. She warned him when I was coming. So their whole conversation was a fake.

I should
have guessed
it when they
talked about the
goldfish.

My brothers could
be mean and rotten. But
they weren't *that* rotten.

Now I understood it. They were in
on it together.

I called Mila after breakfast. She couldn't
come with me to Elm Park.

"I have that piano recital, remember?"

I tried calling Joey, and Kim, and Ralphie.
They were all out or busy with other
things. I guess I'd have to go to Elm Park by
myself. I read for a while in my room.
My dad asked if I wanted to go to the
hardware store. I wasn't interested. My
mom said she had grocery shopping to do.
"Everybody's out, except for Billy. He'll
keep an eye on you."

I looked at my clock. It read 11:32. I'd been reading for almost an hour! I got up, brushed my teeth, and found my oldest brother. "I'm going for a bike ride," I told him.

"Nope," he answered.

"What?"

"You're not going anywhere," he said. "Mom told me to watch you."

"Come on! I've got to be somewhere!"

"Tough."

It wasn't like him to be so mean. That's when I realized that it was all an act. Billy didn't want me to disappear — just in case I wasn't smart enough to figure out the mystery. So I winked and said, "Would you give me a ride . . . to Elm Park?"

Billy smiled. "I was wondering when you would figure it out."

We pulled into Elm Park at exactly noon. "So, where to, detective?" Billy asked.

I stretched my neck, searching for blue balloons. "There." I pointed. "Go that way."

We drove past the swimming pool. Along the way, I saw blue balloons tied to trees and bike racks.

Billy stopped the car at the far end of the park, beside the basketball courts. A huge white sheet dangled between two trees, blowing in the wind. In big red letters it read:

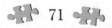

HAPPY BIRTHDAY, JIGSAW!

Everyone was there. All my friends — Reginald, Joey, Ralphie, even Mila! She had been in on it, too. Hillary was there, Daniel and Nick, and Grams. There was a big picnic table set up with yummy food. My dad was at a grill, wearing an apron that read *Kiss the Cook!* My mom stood beside him, smiling at me.

Everybody cheered.

They sang that song that everybody sings on birthdays — *cha, cha, cha!* — even though my birthday was still five days away. I guess that was part of the skeleton's surprise.

"You got me!" I confessed.

Later on, after cake and treats and wild soccer games, my parents came up to me. "Are you happy?" my mother asked.

"Even though it's not Ike and Tina's Laser

Tag and Putt-Putt Emporium?" my father added.

They actually looked worried.

"Happy?" I asked. "Are you kidding? This is the best birthday surprise ever. I can't believe you did all this!"

My father laughed. "We had a lot of help."

"Yeah, Daniel, Nick, Hillary —"

"— and Mila, Joey, Reginald —"

My father said, "And don't forget Ms. Gleason and Mr. C!"

"They were in on it, too?" I asked.

My mother nodded.

My father looked at the ground, then back at me. "I'm sorry, Jigsaw, about the Laser Tag. I know it was what you really wanted. But sometimes —"

I waved my hand. "Who needs that stuff? This is way better!"

"Hey, Jigsaw," Hillary called. "Come on. It's time to open presents!"

I didn't have to be asked twice.